GIANLUCA PIREDDA

WICKED GAME

ENGLISH TRANSLATION AND ADAPTATION
BY

MICHAEL HUDSON

I0533019

RAVEN'S HEAD
PRESS

NEVER SAY NEVERMORE

NEVER SAY NEVERMORE

First Edition • July 2015 • Editing, arrangement and presentation of English language edition is copyright © 2015 Gianluca Piredda and Michael Hudson • Raven's Head Press. All rights reserved.

Italian Edition • July 2015 • copyright © 2015 Gianluca Piredda. First Italian Edition • 2013

English Edition Editor: Christi A. Clore
Cover Design: GPStudios

Gianluca Piredda and Michael Hudson are represented by Tiziana Marzano, literary agent.

PUBLISHERS NOTE

Raven's Head Press
Ravensheadpress.com
ISBN-13: 978-0692466247 • ISBN-10: 069246624X

I want to thank Tiziana Marzano, my agent, because without her this story would not exist; and Michael Hudson, my publisher and a great friend.

This is for my family, an important part of my life. And, of course, all of you, because we write stories for you.

—Gianluca Piredda

Per Gianluca, un buon amico in qualsiasi lingua!

—*Michael R. Hudson*

FOREWORD

Gianluca Piredda has made a name for himself as one of Italy's hottest thriller authors. His stories are memorable and riveting, and his new novelette *Wicked Game* is no exception. A fast and furious thriller, comparable to some of Dean Koontz's best work, *Wicked Game* is packed with twists and turns, and is without question certain to help Piredda multiply his fan base.

After receiving a mysterious phone call in the middle of the night, an ordinary man is offered a single clue to his demise: a photograph of the stranger who aims to kill him. Terrified yet curious, he begins a page-turning joyride that never lets up and keeps the reader glued until the satisfying conclusion. And perhaps the best part of *Wicked Game* is that American readers will finally have a chance to relish in Piredda's fantastic tale, as the American publisher, Raven's Head Press, will be translating his work into English for the very first time.

Do yourself a huge favor and read this terrific novel — you will not be disappointed!

—Michael Laimo
Author of *Deep in the Darkness* and *Dead Souls*

INTRODUCTION

The summers are hot and lazy in Sardinia. The best time to write stories are while sipping iced tea between a dive and swim in the crystalline water of the Mediterranean Sea. The summer of 2012 was particularly warm and it had almost drawn to a close. At that time my comic book with Chuck Dixon and Ben Dunn, *Airboy*, was still shipping in the stores and I was releasing various interviews with the Italian media. I was tossing around some new projects that would materialize shortly thereafter. However, there were empty times and lazy hours spent in the waning days of that summer. My agent, Tiziana Marzano, always the go-getter, proposed to me that I get back into writing short stories. I've never given much time and thought to short stories. I like them, I of course read them, and I have written them, but my body of work has just seemed to take another path. So my output of short story work is relatively small compared to the whole of my published work.

The result of Tizania's push was *Wicked Game*, the novelette you hold in your hands. The ultimate goal was to collect some of my older stories along with some newer ones to create an anthology that will be coming out soon. The idea of this version of *Wicked Game* came to me as I was thinking about music. I wanted to do a "single" sort of like the old vinyl seven-inch 45 rpm records from long ago. The single would contain two sides but in my case I saw this as an opportunity to bring *Wicked Game* to two audiences, the original

Italian version and the translated and adapted to English version by Michael Hudson of Raven's Head Press. This would be a preview of my upcoming anthology, *Forgotten Tales.*

I think this summer of 2015 is the perfect time to present *Wicked Game* to you. I wrote it in the summer, to pass the time while waiting to start new projects and I would be more than happy to help you pass your days on the beach by spending time with the story of Tom Tucker the night he received a mysterious phone call...

—Gianluca Piredda

I was asked by my Italian pal, Gianluca Piredda, to translate his novelette *Wicked Game* into English and if happy with the results to publish it through my boutique publishing house, Raven's Head Press. Always open for new challenges and the opportunity to publish new work I took on the assignment. I had no idea what to expect other than my knowledge that Gianluca is a very fine writer.

I dug into the translation and I have got to be truthful in saying that I was hooked on the first two lines of the translation that read: "Bad news always comes in moments of calm, when you least expect it. It's like some kind of a wicked game of fate, but the truth is bad omens just seem to expect you to be in a state of total relaxation before they break into your life." It just got better from there. It seemed Gianluca was channeling Rod Serling and how could that be a bad thing? It wasn't.

In all translations the translator has to walk a fine line in bringing another author's work into a different language. Some things work and some don't. Gianluca was kind enough to allow me to interject some components into the English version that Italians will not find in their version. That is not to say that the storyline has been changed. It has not. But it has been enriched from an editorial standpoint and from a language standpoint to reach an English speaking audience.

Both works are outstanding. It has been my honor

and great pleasure to work side by side with Gianluca and I can't wait for our next venture together.

—Michael R. Hudson

GIANLUCA PIREDDA

WICKED GAME

ENGLISH TRANSLATION AND ADAPTATION
BY
MICHAEL HUDSON

GIANLUCA PIREDDA
MICHAEL HUDSON

WICKED GAME

ENGLISH EDITION

Bad news always comes in moments of calm, when you least expect it. It's like some kind of a wicked game of fate, but the truth is bad omens just seem to expect you to be in a state of total relaxation before they break into your life. It doesn't matter if it is pouring down rain or if the sun is hot enough to crack rocks, the important thing to bad news when it comes one's way is that it catches you when everything is calm, quiet and you're at peace with yourself and the world. You are, somehow, never prepared for the fateful phone call when it comes.

Tom Tucker knew that.

That night it rained.

The phone made three long rings, while Tucker opened the refrigerator searching for something cold to drink. He located a bottle of San Pellegrino, grabbed it, and took it with him to pick up the receiver.

He was prepared to answer a call from his wife, Trisha, with the most romantic 'hello' he had in his repertoire. He was sure it was her calling.

Her parents had recently arrived in the city and she was doing a whirlwind tour with them of New York City's finest tourist sites. There was plenty to see and one weekend would not be enough. He knew that Trish would take them to eat at Central Park's Tavern On The Green. That was a special place to Tom and to Trisha.

It was there that Tom had given her an orchid, Trish's favorite flower, and linked to the flower was a diamond ring that he had bought her only a few hours before. It was there that he proposed, and more importantly to Tom, that she gave him the 'yes' that would forever change his life.

She was probably calling just to let him know that she'd be late because of the rain and the difficulty in finding a taxi.

Tom picked up the receiver and said, "Hello to the most beautiful girl in the whole wide world!"

The line was quiet for a couple of beats and it wasn't Trisha but a man's voice that replied, "Hello, Tom Tucker."

Tom's initial thought was that he'd just made a total fool of himself but the thought was fleeting as the voice continued without waiting for a reply.

The man on the other end of the phone line spoke slowly and what he had to say sounded confusing and unreal to Tom's ears. He said, "I can show you a photograph of the man who is going to kill you."

The water bottle slipped from Tom's hand.

And suddenly all the calmness was gone from Tom's life.

The gentle rain against the windows now became a violent hammering on the panes as well as inside his head. White flashes of electricity lit up the windows followed by the boom of thunder. Tom's temples began to pulse, his stomach turned to knots as his breath became ragged and seemed to stick in his throat.

The water bottle lay on its side, empty; Tom ignored the cool dampness under his bare feet. The man's words hung in his mind and they would not let go.

"I can show you a photograph of the man who is going to kill you."

"What the..." Tom exclaimed, "Is this some kind of gag?"

"You just dropped a bottle of San Pellegrino and now you are standing in it," came the reply.

It had to be a joke, right, how could it be anything else thought Tom. Why am I wasting time with this asshole? Hang up . . . just hang up the bloody phone. Trish will be home soon, I'll tell her about it, we'll have a few laughs, watch a movie, and go to bed.

But Tom didn't hang up and the man on the other end of the line seemed to read his mind.

Tom silently listened as the deep smooth voice said, "Don't do anything stupid, Tucker. Listen to me and follow my directions to the letter. Do you understand? Answer me Tucker."

"Yes, I ... I understand but who the hell—"

"Shut up Tucker and listen! You meet me at the Lenox Lounge at 288 Lenox Avenue. That's in Harlem,

Tucker. You be there at eight o'clock sharp. Ask for Mac at the bar. Do you understand me Tucker?"

"Yeah . . . I got it, the Lenox Lounge."

There was a click and the line went dead.

Tom Tucker didn't frequent bars. And he wasn't quite sure why he made the forty-five minute drive in pouring down rain to show up at the Lenox. He just made it too. It was seven fifty-eight when he walked in the door.

The place was packed with people. Maybe that's why 'Mac' picked it, to go unnoticed. Tom could hear the hum of the air handlers above the din of the crowd but the air was still thick with ribbons of blue-tinged smoke. A potpourri of perfumes, colognes, sweat and alcohol hung in the air like a wet blanket.

Tom made his way to the bar and when he finally got one of the bartenders to look his way he ordered a beer and casually asked for Mac.

The bartender opened a Heineken, sat in down on a napkin, took the five Tom handed him and motioned with his head to the end of the bar. He turned to another customer. There was no glass offered and no change either.

Tom saw a man sitting by himself at the very end of the bar close to the kitchen entrance. He wore a tan trench coat and he sported a dark gray felt hat that shadowed his face. He was still wet which meant he hadn't been there long. He smoked and though the cloud mingled with all the other smoke in the room it seemed to hang over the man in an ominous fashion obscuring a face that had been wizened by years of hard living.

Tom picked up his beer and went around to approach the man.

"Excuse me, are you . . . uh, are you Mac?"

The man may have looked at him but if he did it was impossible to tell because his head didn't move and with the shadow and smoke he could just as well have been the Invisible Man.

But the man did speak and it was the same voice as on the phone. He said, "Glad you could make it Tucker."

The man had his hands covering a photograph that lay on the bar. He slid the photograph over towards Tom who looked down at it without touching it.

"This is the guy...?" Tom asked flaunting a complacency he had left at home, over an hour ago.

The man nodded.

Tom picked up the photo. His hands were shaking, but Mac seemed to be giving him the photo and he figured since he'd come this far he might as well continue the game, whatever it was. He sighed as he looked at the obviously candid headshot of an average guy with a round face and a rosy-colored complexion. The photo captured the guy in a semi-profile pose, his head awkwardly to one side. Was it taken this way to make it easier to distinguish the small upward pointed nose and that annoying grin? Tom thought the guy resembled a pig. At any other time he would have found the photo to be funny but at that moment he couldn't see anything funny about it. What he saw was the face of a fat man who according to Mac here wanted him dead. The only sensible question was: "why?"

"I don't know..." said Tom, in the hope that the man with the still dripping hat would tell him that it was all a big misunderstanding or even some kind of gag. "I don't understand why this man, whoever he is, would want me dead. I've done nothing wrong!"

"I know," confirmed the mysterious interlocutor, as he pulled another puff of smoke deep into his lungs. "In fact, he was hired by us to kill you."

"What?" Tom started to turn, driven by a fit of rage that faded immediately after the man calmly nodded and said, "Look, no one has anything against you Tucker. My friends and me, we made a bet. We wondered what kind of survival instinct a good man like you possesses. Oh, we've had our eyes on you for awhile and we've observed much, you know."

The man's words, while repulsive to Tom, also seemed to tickle his ego deep down inside. And yet he remained unabashedly puzzled. The man called Mac continued, "You have a beautiful wife, you lead a simple life despite your wealth. We could not find anything against you. Not even things you think others don't know about you. We know . . . and what we know is that you are valued and appreciated by your wife, your friends, and your co-workers. Hell, you're a man to be admired Tucker. So you see, you are perfect..."

"Perfect for what?" Tom knew that the answer would not be one he liked, but he still had to ask.

"For our little game," the man replied, as if speaking of one the most natural things in the world.

"A game ... you pay someone to kill me and you and your cronies call it a game?"

"Listen to me, it's not as you think. I'm giving you a

way out." He motioned to the bartender who brought two shots over.

The man thanked the waiter with a nod, handed him a five and then pushed one of the shots over to Tom.

Both men picked up the drinks and took them down fast. Tom winced and sat his glass down hard. A couple of people at the bar looked his way. Mac smiled and nodded to the onlookers as if to say don't pay any attention to him.

The tension was rising. Tom was to be the point guard of a game that he didn't want any part of and still he didn't know the rules of the game. He had no idea how or when the game would begin and, most importantly, who would win. In fact he didn't care. All he wanted was to turn around, leave the Lenox Lounge, go home, and forget this ever happened. But he couldn't: somewhere out there was a fat-faced pig ready to score points with Tom's life. At the moment he was trapped and he figured it was worth his time to wait and let the man with the hat continue his story. So it was. The man wiped his mouth with a white handkerchief and went on.

"You see, I told you that my friends and I are interested in understanding how a good man like you so attached to your education and principles can crumple when you are placed in a life or death survival situation. And to find out we've hired a killer to stalk you, to torment you in a cat and mouse game, until we tire of it and you're dead. I showed you his photograph to level the playing field a bit. Now you know someone is after you and will eventually kill you and you know exactly what he looks like. It is up to you to decide if you will surrender to your eventual fate, or will you rebel and kill before being killed.

I assure you there is no deception with regards to you. Indeed ... the only one who is being deceived is the killer himself, who does not know of our little meeting. It's perfect, don't you think?"

The man let out a hearty laugh. Tom did not feel like laughing and instead he just stood and stared at the man. Anger welled up within him and his voice cracked a bit as he said, "You ... and your club of friends ... you're all crazy! Do you not realize the absurdity of this situation? If it's a joke, it's time to let me in on it, laugh together, and end it!"

The man stood up to leave not at all worried by the tone of Tom's voice and his words. As he turned he stopped short and blew a long trail of smoke upwards.

"You are free to believe or not to believe my story. If you want you can go to the police, but they will not believe you. The only advice I can give you is to keep your eyes open: the killer is not that far away from you. It's a matter of days, perhaps only hours. Keep your eyes open: the stakes are high. It is your life at stake."

Tom Tucker remained standing as he watched the man lower the brim of his hat and walk away. He watched him disappear into the crowd and leave the crowded room. The last words from Mac were like ice. Tom still held the photo of his to be killer between his index finger and thumb. How would this . . . game change his life? Will he be the victor or would it cost him his life?

When Tom got home if was after eleven and Trisha was already in bed. He had never lied to his wife, but this time he had to do it. He couldn't go to her and tell her that he had spent the last few hours in a bar talking to a guy who called himself Mac talking about Tom's own pending murder. The thought of lying to Trish made him feel sick but there was no way he could burden her with this kind of fantastical, horrific news.

He took off his shoes and wet clothes in the bathroom and crept into the room quietly, on tiptoe, putting his coat on a chair next to his side of the bed, he sat on the mattress.

"Bad day?"

He turned. Trisha stretched. She was sleepy and beautiful in her black negligee. Tom smiled, looking down at the girl who held the key to his heart. The hairs on the back of his neck stood up as he realized he would have to answer her questions. And that he would have to betray her trust. That made it difficult to look into her eyes.

That guy Mac was right about one thing. Tom Tucker was a good man. His wife adored him and he loved her back. Every little gesture of sincerity was a betrayal, even a lie to protect her. There was no malice in his heart but it was still a secret and as such it created a small sense of alienation from the woman he loved so dearly.

"Wyatt screwed things up in the newsroom. There was a huge problem with photos, we were on a deadline, and he told me to take a flying leap—"

"Sweetheart, you know how typical these matters are at the newsroom. They come one minute and then they are over with the next. It's just the pressure of working under such demanding time constraints. It affects all of you. Hey . . . it's over. You know you need to learn to let them unravel these matters on their own," she said, caressing his back.

Tom's excuse did hold roots. Wyatt was known to be a troublemaker and Tom had done him unlimited favors bailing him out time and time again. And there really was an altercation with him at work today.

He was certain that the lie, no, really a partial truth would cover Trish's curiosity but he knew it would probably lead to him having to invent another lie and this annoyed him. The castle stood on the foundation stones on which it was built and frankly his story to Trish was one he didn't like even if it was the only thing he could do.

In response he shrugged.

He stretched his neck from side to side to undo the stress and lay down.

Trisha approached his side of the bed.

"Poor baby. Come here and cuddle with me," she said.

Trisha took him in her arms and rolled him on to herself. Tom kissed her long and deep. His biceps flexed and his back arched as he entered into the depths of her womanhood. He did it as if it were the last time; as if it were the source of a long life that now waned; the panacea to a profound evil that came from the soul. And it worked.

For a moment he forgot the man with the hat and his poisonous cloud of smoke. He forgot about the fat-faced pig and that photograph he had in his jacket's breast pocket. He forgot about the thought of dying at the hands of a whacked out stranger and of having to find a way out of this mess. He also put away his lie to Trish. All these things became distant thoughts as he held and made love to his beautiful and willing wife.

He rolled her on top. Trish's skin held the scent of almonds and it intoxicated him, as her long black hair cascaded down on to his chest. She leaned forward and he took her earlobe between his lips and kissed her neck, the better to smell the scent of her perfume.

The lovemaking eased his anxiety and the tightness in his stomach became less as she carried him far away from his troubles. His breathing increased rapidly but it was in harmony with Trish's. Afterward his heart slowed and a sense of peace came over his being.

Tom would have loved to die right then because the serenity of the moment was so intense and he could not imagine a better place if not beside her.

"Damn, that was good," she purred. "You know you force me into having such a potty mouth at times my husband."

She kissed him deeply, long, and hugged him. A strange force ran through Tom's veins and it led him to hold her tighter. Trisha did not mind; she groaned with pleasure.

Tom's thoughts to himself were not true: he could die now but he would not do it with serenity. He didn't want to die because he wanted many more of those special moments with Trish. He was just thirty-six and he still deserved a lifetime of kisses from her. He wanted to live as many years as God would provide with this woman by his side. Whatever she did made him smile and brought peace into his existence. He had promised her long ago that he would never abandon her and that meant he was not going to let a killer make him break his word.

That night Tom Tucker did not sleep at all. He made love, as he had never done before. The horrible truth was it could be for the last time. Tom planned to live, but he took for granted that defeat might come his way. He wondered if this evening was like the last meal of the accused before the dawn comes ... that final night of perfect calm before the harbinger of bad news comes knocking at one's door. In the dark, now, he wasn't afraid. His thoughts were far away. In his mind there was only Trisha, his Trisha and he could think of nothing better to carry him through the hours of darkness.

The next morning the rain had stopped and the serenity that Tom had felt during the night had evaporated along with it. Some loud beeps and a passing siren awakened him. He was too sleepy to understand if it was an ambulance or the police. Maybe it was a fire truck.

He and Trisha lived in a loft on the Upper East Side and those sounds were a part of life. He had grown to love them. They made him feel alive for, at least, a few more hours. He sighed and stood up; he didn't want to ruin a new day thinking about the events of yesterday. A hot shower and a good breakfast was what he needed.

Tom looked down at Trisha who slept soundly, a

slight smile on her lips, her raven hair awash over her pillow and ivory shoulders. From his nightstand he removed a small notepad and with a red pen wrote, *I love you Trish* on a slip and placed it on her nightstand.

The sun was just breaking. Tom walked out onto the terrace, as was his usual routine as soon as he got up. He leaned against the railing near the wisteria that dominated the building. He enjoyed watching the city wake up and the bustle of people starting their day.

He saw a couple of guys he went to school with many years ago.

There was that couple across the street who kissed goodbye on their doorstep every morning, reminding him of his own closeness with Trish.

He saw Mrs. Harris who was determined to drive her car despite her ninety-two years of age. She was half blind and certainly a public danger and yet she drove and somehow always seemed to make it back home safely.

And then there was the fat man with the bulldog.

Tom paused and shook his head. It was him! The man in the photograph was walking quietly near Central Park, just below his house, with a dog on a leash as ungainly as his owner. God's truth it was the man, no, the killer and he was keeping an eye on the building; he was there for Tom . . . to obtain that damn bloody point that would lead him to victory. Hell, the man probably knew he was being observed. He was a brazen one, full of confidence.

Tom stepped away from the terrace railing and went back inside. He went straight to the bathroom and took the hottest shower he could stand followed by a freezing cold sixty-second count under the spray. Yes, he was wide-awake.

Many of his stories were born under the sharp massage of the shower. That rhythmic cadence on his body relaxed him, it helped him to refocus on the agenda or objective he had ahead of him.   But on occasion it just brought him back down memory lane, to cycle through all the quiet moments of his life. At that moment he thought of only one thing: how to get rid of his persecutor. Mac, the mystery man with the hat was right: he was playing lead. The guy with a face like a pig and the bulldog in tow was not aware of that secret appointment; he did not know Tom was now playing the wicked game too.

He turned off the water and stepped out.

He put on his multicolored terrycloth bathrobe that Trish had given him for Christmas last year and opened the door. She was there waiting for him. She threw her arms around him and kissed him.

"Now move, let me in: it's late! You let me sleep in lover boy," she said, laughing.

Tom stopped her for a moment, holding her in his arms. He gave her another kiss and went back to the bedroom.

His playful wake up note to her lay on the center of the bed. Tom picked it up.   On the back of his note she had written, *I do not ever want to lose you. Never forget that.*

And how could he have forgotten? It was just for her that he had such a great desire to live; a lust for life that he had never felt before she came into his life, even in the year in which he had served as a war correspondent in Afghanistan. The most dangerous period of time he'd ever experienced and yet he spent it with total peace of mind knowing Trish was waiting for him back home.

Tom dressed quickly and went out.

The air smelled of wet earth mixed with exhaust fumes and dampness still permeated the air even though it had stopped raining several hours earlier.

Manhattan traffic was more frantic than usual, so Tom decided to forego the car and take the Lexington Avenue subway. The car was, as usual, packed; fortunately the stops before he needed to get off were few; so he sat deep in thought ignoring the heat and stench of stale air that came with wall-to-wall people. His time was precious and there might be very little of it. Tom was determined to find a solution to his problem and he was certain that the *Paradise For the Do-It-Yourselfer* as he recited the brochure in his hand, would have exactly what he needed.

Tom found his mind kept drifting to his would be killer and the overwhelming anxiety it was beginning to create made him feel as if he were going crazy. He had to pull himself together and concentrate on a plan and on a determination that he would beat his adversary with his own cunning and ingenuity.

He closed his eyes and took a deep breath. The intake of stale air caused him to grimace in disappointment. He took from his pocket a smartphone and opened up a photo of Trisha. It had been taken yesterday while she was showing the city to her parents; just before she returned home, and it had a voice message that went along with it. She said she would be home soon and that she loved him. Trish took great photos. And in this one she was as beautiful as always, with that shy smile and those sincere eyes that could look right into his soul.

She wore jeans and one of his Yankee jerseys. It was big on her and the neck opening uncovered one of her delicate shoulders. But her long raven hair that smelled so good to him cascaded over the shoulder giving her a look of childish whimsy. Tom viewed it as a demonstration of how elegance was something people carried inside them and that it often went hand in hand with simplicity. Tom smiled knowing Trisha was like that . . . elegant and simple ... all at the same time.

Tom's daydream was short lived. He put the smartphone in his pocket and exited the car at 86th Street. He took in a deep breath of underground city air, climbed the stairs and was once again in sunlight. Two cross streets to the north he'd find Dixon Hardware.

The brochure lived up to its promise: the place was truly paradise for the do-it-yourselfer and Tom felt like a kid in a candy shop. Not that he was a DIY enthusiast, but the rummaging distracted him. The dusty product laden shelves of Dixon Hardware stimulated his mind and Tom found it was hard not to smile as he passed row after row of cool man toys.

The shed was full of people, which was normal on a Sunday morning. Tom knew that no one would remember him in such a crowd. There were so many faces, and all different. The isles were full of people who just wanted to stay indoors in anticipation of more rain, taking the opportunity to see new faucets and showerheads, pick out a paint color for their dining room, or tools for renovation work. And then there was Tom, who found himself looking for a tool that would serve to take out an enemy he had never met face-to-face before.

As Tom wandered his mind began to formulate a plan but his thoughts were suddenly interrupted as the hair on the back of his neck stood up. It was Sunday. What if he ran into someone who knew him? What if it were someone from the newsroom? He kept his head down as if interested in every item he passed. Thank God he had remembered to put on a baseball cap, the navy blue cap with a white interlocking "NY" logo. For all intents and purposes he was just a hesitant customer wandering around without knowing exactly what to buy. But he had forgotten one thing. It was for customers just like him that salespeople existed.

"Can I help you?"

Tom jumped. He looked up sheepishly to see a twenty-something guy with orange-red hair, freckled wearing that bright red vest emblazoned with the store's logo on the back and chest pocket. The young man wore a smile that would light up a dark room.

"Uh ... excuse me, I was lost in thought," Tom muttered thinking how stupid he must have sounded. After all his tricks to appear anonymous and then to get caught from behind by a salesman straight out of "Happy Days". He thought to himself: "Yes, I need some kind of improper weapon. What do you recommend?" But then opted for a " I've got a lot of building to do. I am thinking a hammer and nails will wear my hand out."

The clerk smiled: he had the solution.

"Of course! We have just what you need sir. You should try a nail gun, then."

"You mean . . . I can actually try a gun, er, a nail gun . . . here, for practice?"

"Sure! They're perfect for the professional or amateur carpenter. They do look like guns and they will let you do your job in less than half the time."

At the word 'gun' Tom came very close to bursting out with, "I'll take it!" but he caught himself just in time.

"Come on, let me show them to you," continued the clerk.

Tom was already in the right department, which made him seem less clumsy.

The clerk pointed to a large selection of various sized nail guns. Some looked like tools but others were more ominous and appeared more like weapons. "Sir, what material will you be working with? Hardwood, steel, concrete . . .?"

"Oh, I . . . uh, need something very powerful. I need full penetration in rapid succession. It's a huge job!" Tom could hardly believe he just used those words to the smiling clerk.

"I'm gonna guess you need a powder-actuated tool Sir. Hilti is the name brand I would suggest. The technology behind it is a controlled explosion created by a chemical propellant charge, very similar to the process that discharges a real firearm. These come in both a low and high velocity model. The high velocity model will shoot a 75 millimeter bullet-head nail anywhere from 315 feet per second to 1,295 feet per second depending on the type round you are using. They work as a single shot or on fully automatic.

"Do I need some kind of compressor and what about safety? You said these things can fire on automatic?"

"We do have air-actuated nail guns but they are not near as powerful as the powder-actuated guns. Based on what you told me it sure seems you want the most powerful tool we have. As for safety, these things are made to meet all OSHA safety regulations and as such they have a muzzle safety interlock. That means the muzzle has to be pressed against something to make it fire. In automatic mode, you just barely bump it and it will churn out rounds like a Gatling gun." The clerk led him one isle over, stood on tiptoe and pulled from a top shelf a large box with the name Hilti on it. He placed it on the shelf in front of them and opened it to reveal a tool that resembled a cross between a power drill and space-age machine gun.

"Look. Isn't this a beauty?" The young man's tone was that of car salesman, not less charismatic.

But the young man was right. Even Tom saw it. The weapon, no, the tool was a thing of beauty. And once again Tom was lost in thought. He wondered if the nail gun could really be useful to him for protection, for defense . . . and he desperately wanted to be away from there. He could be in church with Trisha and her parents, instead of planning the murder of a man who supposedly had every intention of murdering him.

"Sir? Whaddya think?"

Tom shook his head and looked back at the salesclerk. "Ah yeah, it's a great looking tool. But you said I could try one to see how it works, right?"

"Oh yes sir! You sure can. This one isn't charged but

we do have one fully charged for training and sample purposes. It is in the back. We have a safe enclosure where you put your arms through a Plexiglass wall hole to shoot into a target area. It keeps both you and other customers safe. Follow me."

The young man, believing he had a sale, took up the Hilti nail gun and motioned Tom to follow him to the back of the store through a set of swinging double doors that led the warehouse. And there stood the Plexiglass enclosure under a row of bright florescent lights.

The clerk showed Tom how to unlock the safety and how to trigger the gun on both the single-nail and automatic firing. He then swept his hand back indicating to Tom it was his turn to try the tool. Tom paused. He asked, "didn't you say the tool had to be pressed to something to fire? I don't see anything but a target ten feet away."

"Uh, yes sir, that's right. I did say that and technically it's true. But in order for customers, like you, seeking a powerful, full penetration tool we want you to see what this baby can really do. If you take one hand and pull back the muzzle slide and pull the trigger with the other hand you will see what I mean."

Tom stuck his arms through the rubber-lined holes and picked up the nail gun. It was heavy, the frame being made of what looked like mostly steel with a minimum of plastic accouterments. Tom's hands held a slight tremor as he held the gun and aimed it towards the old-fashioned yellow, red, black, and blue bulls-eye target.

"Don't be shy," said the clerk his face all grins, "let

'er rip!"

Tom squeezed the trigger and the three and a half inch silver nails flashed out of the nail gun faster than the eye could see. He could hear them pinging off the back wall as they slammed into the Plexiglass. He actually did manage to hit the target. The tiny holes were visible but the nail heads were not. The nails had penetrated the target and were deep into the hay bale it was attached to.

"Good job sir! Try it on single shot." The young man walked up and indicted to Tom that he should move the black catch from the rear position to forward with his thumb. Tom did as instructed and fired the nail gun once again. The gun spat out single shots one at a time to each pull of the trigger and he noticed that his control seemed much better. He nailed the target on every shot. Heck, he even managed to place several within the yellow circle of the bulls-eye. Tom looked back around at the sales clerk who still grinned from ear to ear. Tom's mind was already hunting his adversary but he was able to voice, "Thank you. I'll take it."

"Excellent, and a great choice sir! Let me fix you up with rounds and nails and you'll be good to go," said the clerk with great satisfaction. This was his big day. An $1800.00 sale and he wouldn't have to do anything for the rest of the week.

"I'll need a tool belt as well."

"Yes, sir! Thank you sir!"

Tom paid at the checkout, nodded to the sales clerk who had followed him to the front of the store chattering away about how these same nail guns had been used in a lot of films as weapons, and walked away with his briefcase and his new tool. Damn he thought. Why, why did he have to ask questions and then test the stupid thing? Why hadn't he just kept his mouth shut and bought a nail gun? That kid is going to remember me for a long time thought Tom. I could not have been any more conspicuous and he even talked about using them as weapons. He seemed to be reading my mind.

Nobody would stop him and no one would become suspicious but Tom chose to take a taxi up to Madison. He wanted fresh air and, at least for the moment, to immediately flush that fat-faced porcine man out of his conscious mind as if to make the mission he now had ahead of him meaningless.

Tom paid the cabbie and exited the taxi on Madison Avenue, near Central Park. The nail gun was in a plastic bag marked Dixie Hardware and he carried his briefcase in the other hand. Tom was just a guy in a ball cap headed home . . . nondescript and that is just how he wanted to appear. Nobody paid him any attention and he liked that. He even chuckled to himself under his breath. All he had done was to buy a nail gun but suddenly he felt powerful and more in control then ever over his own destiny. To his utter astonishment even the streets of New York seemed safer than usual. Damn, he thought. He would have to go to the hardwood store more often. He was Bob Vila on steroids!

The crowd gave him a sense of anonymity. He was a

part of the flow and yet he was not of them. He could move in the midst of that broad stream of human flotsam unobtrusively, without recognition, and yet at the same time, something deep inside him called out to be noticed . . . but noticed as a man to be reckoned with, a dangerous man, a man who would kill before he would be killed. He became the city and not just a denizen of the city.

Tom had no doubt that 'Pigface' as he had begun to call his adversary in his thoughts would not set up a hit on him in the midst of so many witnesses. No, the fat man would want to pick some place less conspicuous where he would feel safe and less risk to his own well being. It was weird how he felt safer here then the place he would rather be than any other place in the world. He wanted with all his heart to be home with Trish curled up on the sofa with some great jazz playing softly in the background. But for now he had to stay away from his beloved wife. He was being stalked and he could not, he would not bring the stalker near to the woman who gave him hope for a new day.

The flow of pedestrian traffic brought Tom to a Starbuck's and he went inside. He ordered a venti cappuccino, paid, and took it outside to the umbrellaed tables. He sipped the coffee and his eyes scanned the crowd. He missed nothing. Everyone who passed seemed distinct to Tom. He saw eye movement, hands, and what they held. The streets of New York held his protection in the throngs of people and yet they also held his enemy who was somewhere out there quite possibly watching him now, watching and waiting. Tom felt like he was in some sort of surreal Woody Allen film only this film was real life and it could not end well. He just hoped that he would still be alive in the last scene.

It dawned on Tom that he had best be prepared. He had his weapon for what it was worth and it was doing him absolutely no good in the bag. He went back inside the store, made his way to the back, and entered the restroom. Once inside he entered a stall and sat down. He removed the nail gun from the packaging and remembering the detailed instructions from the smiling young sales clerk he assembled the gun, charged it with rounds and nails or in his case ammunition. Then he hung it from the tool belt and stood up. The nail gun hung low just like the old TV gunslingers wore them. His lightweight trench coat covered the ensemble. Tom felt alive. He felt like if the battle for his life were to be fought up close and personal he would, at least, have a chance against Pigface. He took another sip of his coffee. His only fear is that the weight of the nail gun would pull the belt and his pants down to his ankles. Just what he needed, to be a clown, in his *High Noon* moment of life and death. He cinched the belt tighter and it felt more secure even though the gun now rode up higher than it did before. He had to sacrifice being cool for optimum functionality. It was the wise choice. Especially when one's life was on the line.

Tom exited the stall and removed the lid from the trashcan. He pulled out handfuls of used paper and then placed the nail gun box and now waded up store bag into the bottom of the can. Then he covered them back up with all the paper he had removed. Now he was just a guy in a ball cap with a briefcase. But he was armed. Tom exited the restroom with his coffee and walked back outside. It was going to rain again. The sky was darkening and he wind was beginning to whip Central Park's autumn leaves into showers of red and gold that rained on the pedestrians as they made their way through the heart of the city.

Tom took a last sip of his cappuccino, tossed the cup, and resumed his walk in search of his opponent. A few meters from the loft he turned back in the direction of the park. He was certain that if he retraced his steps he would run across Pigface again. If it wasn't today, it would be tomorrow. It was imminent. Death was coming soon to him or his adversary unless the game managers grew tired of the game and somehow he felt they never grew tired of sadistic games. The man called Mac gave no indication that he or his cronies had any sort of concern as to which man won. They just wanted a game.

As Tom walked and scanned the pedestrian traffic, his mind unavoidably began to wander. And as a condemned man's mind will often do at such times, his thoughts turned to what he loved the most and how desperately he did not want to lose that. Guilt crept into his state of mind as he played over the time that he could have, no, he should have redeemed better than he had. Why had he spent so many Sundays writing leaving Trisha to entertain herself? They had talked of many mini-weekend vacations and yet how many had they taken together? They had spoken often of a child together and yet there was still no son or daughter. A revelation came to him. If any good could come of such a perverted game of life and death, it would be that he would now look at every moment with Trisha as precious. He would no longer take the good they shared for granted and it was very good indeed. They had talked of an extended European vacation and of going back to visit her parent's home in Sardinia. No computers, no cell phones, only the two of them and if God was willing and the stars were aligned just right, maybe, just maybe they would come back as a threesome.

He walked through the park that was now thinning as people began to head for shelter from the impending rain. The cool breeze and the walking invigorated Tom's mind. Why had he not taken Trisha walking when their loft was practically across the street from the park? Why did it take the danger of death to make him rediscover the little things that he loved about Trisha were not little things at all? She was important and while they lived and loved together at times it was as if they were miles apart from one another. He knew it was not her fault. Trisha was steadfast in her commitment and in how she dealt with their relationship. She never seemed to waver. It was me who wavered.

Tom stopped and took in a deep breath of air. He touched the nail gun at his side well anchored under his coat. He had a moment's hesitation. What the hell was he doing? Tom never played games, especially games of chance. He just wasn't a gambler. And yet here he was gambling that he would kill his adversary, save his own life, and renew and recommit to the girl he loved. No small task.

His mind drifted back to the extended European vacation with Trisha. He thought they could take it now, perhaps, never to return to the States. As a writer, he could work anywhere. That would have been the wisest decision, right? New air . . . new life, to hell with everything else. They had enough money to start over somewhere else. Anywhere they wanted to go. He could probably use what he was going through right now as the basis for that novel he wanted to write. All well and fine but what he would say to Trisha? He would tell her about the damn phone call? How could he tell her about the Lenox and its smell of sweat mixed with stale beer? Or about that Mephistopheles of a man called simply Mac who, from under the hat, in a cloud of smoke, announced his destiny? How could he possibly share with her that he had spent the morning with a very expensive powder-activated nail gun hidden under his coat ready to take out a guy who, in fact, had not really done anything to him? Not yet, at least. How could he ask her to drop everything and move somewhere because he had been selected among the millions of New Yorkers to be a pawn in a macabre lottery? And who could guarantee that the killer would not follow them wherever they went just to win the bloody, damn game? Pigface was a professional, dammit, and people like him always carry out the mission. Tom knew that wherever they went he would be unearthed, even to the ends of the world. And there is not way he could allow Trisha to take a part in his game. Not as a confederate or as a witness to his own murder. The words seemed to scream in his mind: "She has to stay out! She must stay out! " By now it was almost a mantra with Tom.

"You must stay out," and he placed a trembling hand upon the side of his coat to feel the sidearm.

"You must stay out," and he felt the hard knots in his stomach that racked his guts like a couple of violent fists punching here and there. He had to sit down.

A lonely street saxophonist stood on a corner and improvised the blues. The music made him feel a little like Philip Marlowe. Wow, he'd gone from being in a Woody Allen film to a Raymond Chandler novel. But Tom wasn't Marlowe. Hell, he wasn't even Humphrey Bogart. He was Tom Tucker and, alive or dead, this was his very own special reality.

Tom stopped to listen to the session. The musician was somewhere in his mid-thirties to early forties. He wore baggy brown corduroy pants that obscured his sandaled feet and a grey sweatshirt that had perhaps once been white. The man seemed to know the exact feelings Tom was having and he was very adept into transferring those feelings into notes of pain, anguish, and even remorse. The sax continued to wail it soulful music and Tom walked over and dropped a dollar and some change into the instruments open case. The man nodded his thanks and kept right on blowing his mournful tune.

Tom walked over and slumped into a bench. After a moment he pulled out his smartphone and sent a text message to Trisha.

"Thinking of you."

Seconds later came her response: "Me too. Oops! I thought your text was from someone else." She added a kiss and a smiley emoticon.

Tom had to laugh. They had been playing that silly texting game for years and still he felt a tinge of jealousy mixed in with the fun. Trisha was an incredible beauty and he was a very lucky man to have her as his wife. Tom brought his head back and took note of his surroundings once again. Around him there was life, and this gave him positive feelings. He needed positive feelings as the ever-impending sense of death surrounded him. But from where . . . and when? All Tom knew is that it would be coming.

A young couple, probably on their first date sat two benches away. Laughing, talking, the girl showed the boy the cover of a book she'd just bought him. Clearing his throat, the boy read the opening words with as much masculinity as he could muster. They both giggled at his antics. Tom closed his eyes again and, a moment later, re-opened them to see the couple kissing. He nodded approvingly. Two souls were joining together and it was good.

A mother taking care of her child distracted Tom's attention. The woman parked the child's stroller in front of him. She took the child up in her arms and wiped its nose. She kissed and hugged the small figure. This was another scene and he liked it too. Just two of hundreds of thousands that take place every day. Tom thought that, yes, he would have to return often to Central Park, but not alone. The next time he came, if he was alive to come again, it would be with Trisha. The woman gently placed the child back into the stroller and resumed her walk.

A group of the runners passed. Tom followed them with his eyes. He wondered if he still had the stamina for a run like that. Was it too late to try?

A hand on his shoulder made him snap erect.

"I'm sorry ... I don't want to bother you..." The boy was in his mid-twenties, seemingly just out of college, with a backpack slung over his shoulder and a map of New York City in his hand. He looked like a typical young European tourist.

Tom assured him with a smile, but said nothing.

"I'm on vacation with my girlfriend," he said. A comely girl, shy, a bit sloppy but nice, probably younger than him, looked down and nodded a greeting with her hand. The boy continued, "...and I was wondering if you could take a photograph of us together. Would you mind? We want to have some memories of us together for when we go back to Europe. "

Europe. Yes, Europe. Wasn't he just thinking about taking Trish there for a vacation . . . or was it forever? But the reality of it was he was sitting on a park bench in Central Park waiting to kill or be killed and while he was at it why not just interact with all the tourists and street people. He thought what a grand guy I am. "Northern Europe?" He asked, as he took the boy's digital camera.

"Helsinki," answered the boy. Which justified why his coat was tied around his waist, as if it were a hot spring in New York instead of a brisk fall.

"Have you ever been?"

"No," Tom said, shaking his head. "But if my plans go well, it could be the destination of my next vacation."

"I hope you do well!"

"Count on it!" Tom declared, knowing inside South Italy, most likely Sardinia would be the final choice.

The two kids began posing and Tom snapped several photos.

"Shall I do another?" he asked. He was enjoying himself, or at least lightly amused by the two young tourists. "I'd like for you to take a few home a little of New York, not New Yorkers." Tom looked on the display at how many passersby had been captured with the lens in his photos. He had captured the two young Finns in some delightfully candid poses. They made Central Park and New York beautiful but there was also the drunk who could hardly stand in the background on one shot. And another had the runners in the background. And then Tom almost dropped the camera. The third shot had someone familiar in the background. From behind the young couple he could see a round-faced, bald-headed guy with a rosy-colored complexion being pulled along by a bulldog. In his other hand he held an envelope. It was Pigface. The man was looking right at the camera in the photo. Tom immediately looked up and scanned his surroundings. The man was still there about twenty feet away. He seemed not to be paying any attention to Tom. He just followed the dog's lead and now they were both headed down Madison.

Tom gave the camera back to the boy and apologized for his sudden change in demeanor. "Forgive me, but I just realized that I'm late for an appointment," he said as he quickly started walking away from the couple in the direction of Pigface. Then he turned around and added, "Ah, the third picture is good. Keep the one with you two guys on the bench.

You look great!" The two young Finns watched him walk off. They had not even had time to thank the kind stranger.

After a bit Tom slowed his pace. He didn't want to attract any more attention. He wanted all of his focus to be on his rival but he did not want the man to notice him just yet. Yes, he wanted to make sure that he met the man face to face. Maybe talk to him . . . make him understand that this game could be over with if they would both just quit, quit now . . . a mutual agreement between two sensible adult men who both wanted to live. And, if worse came to worse, Tom would kill the other man before the man had a chance to kill him. But Tom wanted it to be in a more secluded place. Confronting him in front of all these people would do no good at all.

Pigface suddenly stopped. Tom stopped about thirty feet behind him. The man pulled a cell phone from his pocket and answered. He spoke at length, holding the phone with the hand that held the envelope. With the other hand he gestured with difficulty, because of the nylon leash to the ever-moving bulldog. The man looked up from the call, noticed Tom, and quite suddenly his facial expression changed. He dismissed the caller with, "Well, now I have to go." and put the phone back in his pants pocket. Tom looked down at the sidewalk but kept one eye on the man as he resumed his march towards a showdown. He was sweating profusely.

He had been discovered. Now the killer knew that he was aware of everything, and the man was now planning his own counter strategy towards Tom's advance. Tom had to act quickly. He had no time to think. He had to act just as he had that time in Afghanistan, when he found himself at the border with machine guns pointed at him and every mistake could be fatal. He had to think and act instinctively. There could be no screw-ups.

Tom sped up now that he had been discovered. He wanted to reach the man now. The man was sweating and had to slow down his pace almost to a stop pulling the dog along who had stopped to sniff at a fire hydrant. Tom caught up with him in just a few steps. Oddly, the man seemed nonplused at having Tom so close to him. In fact he simply smiled and said hello.

"Hullo! What a day, all this rain!" he said.

Tom looked at the man sternly. Where the hell was this thing going?

"Lucky for me I've got old Tommy here," and the man pointed toward the still sniffing bulldog. Tom still said nothing and stared at the man with icy eyes. The nerve of the bastard! He gave my name to his dog in a sign of contempt for me, a perfect stranger! What the hell!

"You know bulldogs are beautiful beasts. My wife says old Tommy looks like me. But you know, she's really a bitch and not much of a companion with all of her complaining and such. So, whenever I can, I take good old Tommy boy here for a walk."

The dog's name ... and he would die soon. Was this a veiled threat or just an absurd coincidence?

Then the pig-looking man held out his hand.

"Hullo again ... my name is Jeremy Daniel," said the man, who seemed to want to make friends. Tom was hesitant, but he finally managed within himself to reach out to clasp the proffered hand. He shook it and the man's was limp and clammy. Not at all what he had expected from a seasoned hitman.

"So, you don't recognize me?" asked Tom quizzically.

"Should I?" asked the man, who now seemed slightly annoyed.

"I'm the real reason you are out here walking around," Tom said. "My name is Tom Tucker. Journalist. Writer."

Pigface, who now had a name and a surname, only God knows if it was the real one, smiled. "Excuse me ... I am really unforgivable. I am sure that for those who do your line of work it isn't so good not to be recognized in the street. Please forgive me for not recognizing you Mr. Tucker."

Tom felt like an idiot. Passerby looked at him as he stood legs apart in front of Jeremy Daniel. Tom towered over the man. And why was the man so damn docile? Hell, it seemed, even to Tom, that he himself was the aggressor and not the man who was sent to kill him. What did others think?

Jeremy Daniel blinked and then smiled once again. He said, "Well Mr. Tucker, I must be moving along now. Old Tommy boy is chomping at the bit to find the perfect spot to do his business. I hope we will meet again sometime. You know, in my line of work our motto is 'we never meet a stranger'." As he spoke the last line, the man slipped his hand under his jacket to pull something out.

Tom's heart began to beat wildly and his temples

throbbed as his brain exploded with answers even before questions were asked. Strange inner jitters took hold of his legs and he thought he might collapse to the ground. The trilling melody of the tenor saxophone in the distance seemed to Tom like a sort of desperate siren warning that the bombs would be coming, the showdown moment was at hand. It was only a matter of who was faster. Tom put his hand under his coat and pulled out the powerful powder-actuated nail gun. Just as Jeremy Daniel looked up and held his hand out Tom pointed the nail gun at the man's forehead and pressed the trigger as he held back the muzzle slide with his other hand.

TUMB . . . TUMB . . . TUMB ... tumb, tumb, tumb, tumb, tumb

The macabre sound, dull and rhythmic as it picked up speed almost seemed like the staccato drum intro to a seventies rock song. It seemed to interweave in unison with the strident sax whose sound was floating in the distance.

The man's eyes were wide in shock as he gasped once and fell. His forehead held eight three and a half inch sixteen-penny nails buried deep within his brain's frontal cortex.

Jeremy Daniel fell in slow motion, or at least it seemed he did to Tom. He landed on the sidewalk with a muffled thud. His eyes seemed to stare right into Tom's inner being.

Tom dropped the nail gun to his side but still held his finger just above the trigger. Gary Cooper had faced his dreaded enemy and the battle was over. He had won. He would live.

Tommy barked and ran to lick the big sweaty face of his dead master.

A woman shouted. Tom did not look at her or at any of the pedestrians that were now gathering around the grisly scene. He looked down at the man and wondered how it had been that easy to take him . . . a hired killer . . . a mercenary who was going to blow him from the face of the earth. No more Trisha. No more anything. The end.

Tom wanted to see the weapon that Jeremy Daniel was going to use to kill him; the weapon that he was pulling from his pocket as he lured him off balance with his act of the good neighbor and folksy quotes.

Jeremy Daniel held a business card between his fingers. The crumpled paper read 'Jeremy Daniel – Insurer Life, Health, Property.' At the bottom in smaller script was an address, website, and contact details. In eight-point type across the middle of the card was the slogan 'We never meet a stranger.'

Tom did not understand anything. Wasn't the man using a trick of the trade, a tactic to catch him off guard? Wasn't he then going to hit him with perfect calm, once he got my confidence? Certainly this was not the case with Jeremy Daniel. The now deceased Jeremy Daniel. But how could it be that he had killed the wrong person? Was it just an unfortunate coincidence that Daniel resembled the man in the photo he had grown to think of as Pigface?

When Tom was taken he was still standing there with the nail gun in hand hanging by his side. He stood oblivious to anything and everything around him except the corpse lying at his feet.

The New York Times ran a headline the following day that read: 'COHEN TRIAL STAR WITNESS SAL DE BIASE MURDERED' The copy read, *'The star witness of the Cohen mob trial, Sal De Biase was brutally murdered yesterday afternoon in front of a crowd of astonished witnesses.*

We currently do not know the relationship between the deceased, now in the witness protection program, and his attacker, the writer and journalist Tom Tucker, but apparently it was not a settling of mob related scores. Tucker, armed with a powerful nail gun, stalked De Biase and then finished him with eight shots to his forehead. Tucker, in a daze, did not offer any resistance to law enforcement and merely stated that 'the man with the pig face would kill him.'

Sal De Biase, had been in the witness protection program for almost three years now under the name of Jeremy Daniels and was working as a life, health, and property insurance agent.

The Cohen trail is scheduled to resume in January of 2016."

The man pulled down on the brim of his dark gray felt hat and sat his margarita on a marble coffee table. He wiped small beads of sweat from his forehead with a silk handkerchief and reached out to pick up his cell phone when it buzzed. The newspaper he was reading covered his legs like a bedsheet.

A cloud of smoke enveloped the man as he puffed

away on a cigarette. The ashtray on the coffee table was full of butts so he had been there awhile. He looked at the number on the phone's display, and said with a hint of a smile, "You read the paper?" There was an air of victory in his smug tone.

"Yes," replied his companion. "It seems you were right: it worked."

"And none of us will ever be suspected. Officially a madman took out De Biase. A random crime, no motive and no tie with our organization."

"And if Tucker speaks?"

"What's he gonna say? That he was approached by a man who doesn't exist, a guy called Mac? Nah, he won't talk. And it won't matter anyway. His story wouldn't hold up. He is officially insane. Bellevue bound to be sure. I'm just enjoying the sun and sights here in the Cayman Islands."

The two men laughed with satisfaction. After all, they had just won the match in the wicked game of perversion based on doubt, fear, and death.

"Enjoy the sun," said the speaker on the other end of the phone. "Yeah, you should get some sun yourself sometime," he said in a confidential tone. The two laughed again and the man hung up. He stubbed out his cigarette, lit another, and resumed his margarita. He threw the paper to the sand and kept his word: he would enjoy the sun and the sights of the Cayman Islands. After all, who knew when the next game would begin?

THE END

GIANLUCA PIREDDA

WICKED GAME

WICKED GAME

EDIZIONE ITALIANA

Le cattive notizie arrivano sempre nei momenti di calma, quando meno te lo aspetti. È un gioco perverso del destino, ma i brutti presagi aspettano che tu sia in totale relax per irrompere nella tua vita. Poco importa se fuori piove o se c'è un sole in grado di spaccare le pietre. L'importante è che tutto accanto a te sia calmo, tranquillo, e che tu sia in pace con te stesso, impreparato alla fatidica telefonata.

Tom Tucker lo sapeva bene.

Quella notte pioveva.

Il telefono fece tre squilli lunghi, mentre Tucker apriva il frigorifero per versarsi qualcosa di fresco. Non era un bevitore e prese dell'acqua. Portò con sé la bottiglia e si preparò ad accogliere Trisha, sua moglie, con il miglior "ciao" che avesse in repertorio. Era sicuro si trattasse di lei. I suoi parenti erano arrivati da poco in città e stava facendo con loro un giro turistico per New York. C'era molto da vedere e un solo week end non sarebbe bastato. Si sarebbero fermati a mangiare qualcosa in uno dei ristoranti che loro due preferivano. Era lì che Tom le aveva dato un'orchidea, il fiore preferito da Trisha, legata all'anello che le aveva comprato poche ore prima. E fu lì che lei gli disse il suo "sì". Probabilmente voleva avvisare che avrebbe fatto tardi, vista la pioggia e la difficoltà di reperire un taxi.

Rispose.

La voce non era quella di Trisha. L'uomo dall'altro capo dell'apparecchio parlava lentamente e quanto aveva da dire suonava confuso e irreale alle orecchie di Tom. Fu al pronunciare delle parole "posso mostrarti la foto di chi ti ucciderà" che la bottiglia gli cadde di mano.

Tutta la calma di quella serata svanì d'incanto.

La dolce pioggia contro i vetri diventò un picchiare violento. In lontananza gli sembrò persino di sentire dei tuoni.

Le tempie gli presero a battere e una stretta allo stomaco gli faceva inciampare il respiro in gola.

L'acqua infradiciò il tappetto e Tom non badò al fresco umido sotto i piedi scalzi. Tutto quello che gli rimase in testa, fu "posso mostrarti la foto di chi ti ucciderà".

Era sicuramente uno scherzo, non poteva essere altrimenti, e Tom pensò che stava perdendo fin troppo tempo con quello sconosciuto. Avrebbe dovuto riattaccare e chiamare la polizia. Raccontare quella storia assurda, farsi quattro risate e aspettare che Trisha tornasse a casa per guardare un film insieme e mettersi a letto.

L'uomo dalla voce roca e calma pareva leggergli nel pensiero. Gli sconsigliò di fare alcunché, ma di seguire le indicazioni alla lettera.

Tom si azzittì e ascoltò.

Il "No Way" non era il tipo di locale che Tom Tucker era solito frequentare.

Era talmente pieno di gente da poter passare inosservati; l'aria densa di fumo si mischiava all'odore di birra stantia e sudore alcolico.

L'uomo col cappello madido di pioggia tirò una boccata di sigaretta e fece scorrere una foto sopra il tavolo di formica. La nuvola generata gli nascondeva il volto incartapecorito da anni di bionde.

Tom guardò la polaroid senza toccarla.

«È lui?», chiese ostentando una sicumera che aveva lasciato a casa, isolati più in là.

L'uomo annuì.

Tom prese la foto. Le mani gli tremavano, ma lo doveva fare. Tirò un sospiro e vide il primo piano di un tizio dalla faccia tonda e rosea. Il riporto gli copriva maldestramente una parte di testa. Sarà stato per il naso piccolo e all'insù e per via di quel ghigno fastidioso – cosa aveva poi da ridere? – ma il paragone con un maiale venne facile alla mente. In un'altra occasione lo avrebbe trovato anche divertente ma in quel momento non ci vedeva niente di buffo. Vedeva solo la faccia di un uomo grasso che, di lì a poco, gli avrebbe fatto la pelle. L'unica domanda che trovava sensata era: "perché?"

«Non lo conosco...» disse Tom, nella speranza che l'uomo col cappello gli dicesse che era tutto un equivoco. «Non capisco perché questa persona possa volere la mia morte. Non gli ho fatto nessun torto»

«Lo so bene», confermò il suo misterioso interlocutore, mentre tirava un'altra boccata di fumo. «Infatti, è stato assunto da noi per ucciderla.»

«Come?!» Tom fece per alzarsi, spinto da un raptus d'ira che scemò immediatamente dopo un cenno calmo dell'uomo che stava seduto di fronte a lui.

«Ascolti, nessuno ha niente contro di lei. Io e i miei amici abbiamo solo fatto una scommessa. Ci siamo chiesti quanto potesse essere forte l'istinto di sopravvivenza di una brava persona come lei. L'abbiamo osservata molto, sa?» spiegò l'uomo, quasi volesse solleticare l'ego di Tom che rimase impassibilmente perplesso. «Lei ha una bella famiglia, conduce una vita semplice nonostante la sua agiatezza. Non siamo riusciti a trovare nessuna pendenza a suo carico. È una persona stimata e apprezzata. Un uomo da ammirare. Per questo era perfetto.»

«Perfetto per cosa?» Tom sapeva che la risposta non gli sarebbe piaciuta, ma doveva comunque chiederlo.

«Per il nostro gioco», rispose, come se parlasse della cosa più naturale del mondo.

«Un gioco... lei paga qualcuno per ammazzarmi e lo chiama "gioco"?»

«Mi ascolti, non è come pensa. Io le sto dando una via d'uscita.»

L'uomo fece segno al barista che gli portò un boccale di birra. La spiegazione necessitava di un rinforzo.

L'uomo ringraziò il cameriere con un sorriso e un

lento cenno col capo, gli porse un paio di banconote da un dollaro e bevve d'un fiato. La tensione stava salendo. Tom si trovava a essere il playmaker di una partita che non avrebbe voluto giocare e ancora non conosceva le regole del gioco. Non aveva idea di quale sarebbe stato il quadrato di gara e, soprattutto, che cosa avrebbe vinto. In realtà nemmeno gli importava. Avrebbe voluto alzarsi, andare via e dimenticare tutto. Ma non poteva: là fuori c'era un ciccione dalla faccia da maiale pronto a segnare il suo punto. Valeva la pena attendere che l'uomo col cappello si dissetasse e continuasse la sua storia. Così fu. Si asciugò la bocca con un fazzoletto bianco e proseguì.

«Vede, le ho già detto che io e i miei amici siamo interessati a capire quanto una brava persona come lei possa essere attaccato alla vita da lasciarsi alle spalle la propria educazione e i propri principi per far prevalere l'istinto di sopravvivenza. Per questo abbiamo assunto quel killer e per questo le ho mostrato la sua foto. Lei sa che là fuori qualcuno vuole ucciderla, ma sa anche che faccia ha il suo assassino. Ora sta a lei decidere: arrendersi al destino, o ribellarsi e uccidere prima di essere ucciso. Non c'è nessun inganno. Anzi... l'unico a essere ingannato è proprio il killer stesso, che non sa di questa nostra piccola riunione.»

L'uomo rise e Tom non si sentiva per niente sollevato dall'informazione ottenuta. Anzi: la rabbia salì ulteriormente, come il suo tono di voce.

«Lei... e il suo club di amici siete dei pazzi! Si rende conto dell'assurdità di questa situazione? Se è uno scherzo, è il momento di piantarla!»

L'uomo si alzò per niente preoccupato dal tono di

Tom e fece per andarsene. Poi si fermò di colpo e sentenziò.

«Lei è libero di credere o meno a questa storia. Se vuole può andare dalla polizia, ma non le crederebbero. L'unico consiglio che le posso dare è di tenere gli occhi aperti: quell'uomo non è poi così lontano e la colpirà. È questione di giorni, forse solo di ore. Tenga gli occhi aperti: la posta in gioco è alta. È la sua vita»

Tom Tucker rimase in piedi mentre guardava l'uomo sistemarsi la falda del cappello e andare via. Lo osservò sparire tra la folla e uscire dal locale. Non ribatté niente: era come di ghiaccio e teneva la foto per un lembo, tra l'indice e il pollice. Gli avrebbe cambiato la vita. O gliela avrebbe fatta perdere.

Al suo ritorno Trisha era già a letto. Da quando si conoscevano lui non le aveva mai mentito, ma questa volta avrebbe dovuto farlo. Non poteva andare da lei e raccontarle che aveva passato le ultime ore in un locale di periferia a parlare con un tizio senza nome che gli annunciava la sua morte. Si sentiva un verme per questo, ma non poteva fare altrimenti.

Tolse le scarpe in bagno e lì lasciò anche i pantaloni umidi di pioggia.

Entrò in camera senza far rumore, in punta di piedi, appoggiando la giacca su una poltrona adiacente alla sua parte di letto e si sedette sul materasso.

«Giornataccia?»

Lui si voltò. Trisha si stirò. Era assonnata e bellissima nel suo top nero. Abbozzò un sorriso, lo sguardo basso: non poteva guardarla negli occhi mentre stava per tradirla. Tom Tucker era così: per lui ogni gesto di poca sincerità era un tradimento, anche una bugia di quel tipo. Lo avrebbe fatto senza malizia ma era comunque un segreto da cui estraniava sua moglie.

«Wyatt ha combinato un guaio in redazione. Un problema di foto, mi ha chiesto di fare un salto...»

«...e tu ci sei andato. Tipico. Devi imparare a fargliele sbrogliare da solo queste faccende», disse lei carezzandogli la schiena.

La scusa attecchì. Wyatt era noto per essere un casinista e doveva a Tom un numero illimitato di favori. Era certo che lo avrebbe coperto, ma anche a lui non avrebbe potuto dire la verità. Avrebbe dovuto inventare un'altra balla e questo lo scocciava. Il castello di menzogne su cui si stava costruendo quella storia non gli piaceva, ma era l'unica cosa che poteva fare.

Per tutta risposta fece spallucce.

Si tolse la camicia e si stese.

Trisha si avvicinò a lui

«Povero bimbo. Vieni qui che ti coccolo», disse lei.

Prese Trisha tra le braccia e la fece rotolare su di sé, i bicipiti non più allenati come un tempo ma comunque segnati. E la baciò. Lo fece come se fosse l'ultima volta; quasi fosse la fonte di una lunga vita che, ormai, vedeva tramontata; la panacea a un male profondo che veniva dall'anima. Funzionava.

Per un momento dimenticò l'uomo secco col cappello madido e la sua venefica nuvola di fumo; il ciccione dalla faccia da maiale e quella foto che teneva nel taschino della giacca; l'idea di poter morire per mano sua e il dover trovare una soluzione per uscire da quel guaio; anche la balla da inventare per farsi spalleggiare da Wyatt divenne un pensiero lontano. Non era il momento di pensarci. Stava troppo bene tra le braccia di lei.

Il profumo di mandorla della sua pelle lo inebriava, mentre i capelli neri e lunghi gli carezzavano il viso. Le prese il lobo dell'orecchio tra le labbra e le baciò il collo, per sentire meglio il suo profumo.

Quel senso di angoscia che lo accompagnava da qualche ora scompariva. Quella boccia nello stomaco che sentiva sino ad allora si fece meno pesante. Il respiro tornava a fluire lungo le condotte nasali e non abortiva in gola.

Tom sarebbe anche potuto morire in quel momento e lo avrebbe fatto con serenità perché non poteva immaginare un posto migliore se non accanto a lei. Lo pensò e gli scappò ad alta voce.

«Ne dici di fesserie, alle volte» lo riprese. «Mi costringi a tapparti la bocca.»

Lo baciò profondamente, a lungo e lo strinse a sé. Una strana forza attraversava le vene di Tom e lo portava a stringerla più forte. A lei non spiaceva e mugugnò.

Dopotutto non era vero: non avrebbe potuto morire anche in quell'istante e non lo avrebbe fatto con serenità. Non avrebbe voluto morire perché desiderava ancora molti di quei momenti. Aveva trentasei anni e meritava ancora tanti di quei baci. Doveva e voleva vivere molti altri anni con quel metro e sessanta di donna che continuava a dimostrarne ventisei.

Qualunque cosa lei facesse riusciva a farlo sorridere e a rendergli la vita serena. Ed era così anche per lei.

Lui le aveva promesso che non l'avrebbe

abbandonata mai e non aveva intenzione di farlo nemmeno davanti a un killer.

Quella notte Ted Tucker non dormì per niente. Fece l'amore come non l'aveva mai fatto. Poteva essere per l'ultima volta. Era intenzionato a vivere, ma non dava per scontata la sconfitta. Consumò quell'ultimo pasto del condannato a morte prima che le luci dell'alba tornassero a schiarire una calma notte foriera di pessime notizie. Il buio, ora, non faceva paura. I pensieri erano lontani. Nella sua mente c'era solo Trisha. Poteva pensare a qualcosa di meglio?

La mattina smise di piovere. Quella calma pesante della notte prima sembrava essere andata via, Tom Tucker venne svegliato da alcuni forti colpi di clacson e da una sirena che passava. Era troppo assonnato per capire se si trattasse di un'ambulanza o della polizia. Forse erano i Vigili del Fuoco.

Era l'Upper East Side e amava quei suoni. Lo facevano sentire vivo ancora per poche ore. Tirò un sospiro e si alzò: non aveva voglia di rovinarsi la giornata pensando ai fatti di ieri. Ci avrebbe pensato dopo una doccia e una buona colazione, ma ora no: la notte era stata bella e voleva continuare a ricordarla. Quindi si alzò, guardò Trisha dormire, le sorrise con tenerezza e prese un cartoncino color avorio. Scrisse "ti voglio bene" con la penna rossa, quella che lei usava a lavoro, e lo mise sul comodino vicino a lei.

La luce del mattino era meno fioca, ora, e Tom andò in terrazza come faceva di consueto appena si alzava. Si appoggiò alla ringhiera, vicino al glicine che dominava l'edificio. Gli piaceva guardare la gente passare.

I ragazzi che andavano a scuola lo riportavano indietro negli anni.

Quella coppia che si salutava sul portone gli ricordava lui e sua moglie, con i loro riti mattutini.

La signora Harris si ostinava a prendere la macchina nonostante i suoi novantadue anni. Un pericolo pubblico, visto come guidava. Infatti, inchiodò di colpo e ripartì nuovamente a tutta birra.

E poi c'era lui, il ciccione con il bulldog.

Tom si fermò un attimo e scosse la testa. Era lui! L'uomo della fotografia passeggiava tranquillamente nei pressi di Central Park, proprio sotto casa sua, con al guinzaglio un cane sgraziato quanto il proprietario. Lo stava tenendo d'occhio, questo era certo quanto Dio. Si trovava lì per lui, per segnare quel punto maledetto che lo avrebbe portato alla vittoria. Probabilmente sapeva anche di essere osservato. Con tutta sicurezza voleva essere visto.

Tom si allontanò dalla ringhiera della terrazza e rientrò a casa. Si diresse in bagno: ci voleva una doccia.

Molte delle sue storie nascevano sotto i massaggi appuntiti dello scrosciare d'acqua. Quel cadenzare sul suo corpo lo rilassava, lo aiutava a riflettere. O semplicemente lo riportava indietro con la memoria, per passare in rassegna tutti i momenti sereni della sua vita. In quel momento pensava solo una cosa: a come liberarsi dal suo persecutore. Quell'uomo misterioso col cappello aveva ragione: lui giocava di vantaggio. Il tizio con la faccia da maiale e il bulldog al seguito non era al corrente di quell'appuntamento segreto; non sapeva che avrebbero giocato alla pari.

Chiuse l'acqua e uscì.

Infilò il suo accappatoio multicolore e aprì la porta. Trisha era lì che lo aspettava. Gli buttò le braccia al collo e gli diede un bacio.

«Ora spostati, fammi entrare: è tardissimo» disse lei, mentre rideva.

Tom la bloccò per un momento, stringendola tra le braccia. Le diede un altro bacio e tornò in camera.

Sul retro del suo biglietto c'era scritto: "Anche io te ne voglio. Non dimenticarlo mai".

E chi se lo sarebbe dimenticato? Era proprio per lei che aveva una gran voglia di vivere. Una voglia di vivere che non aveva mai sentito, nemmeno nell'anno in cui fece l'inviato di guerra in Afghanistan. Il periodo più pericoloso della sua vita, ma trascorso con una tranquillità assoluta. Subito dopo conobbe lei e pensò che su quella terra ci sarebbe voluto rimanere ancora per tanto tempo.

Si vestì in fretta e uscì.

Qualcosa avrebbe fatto.

L'aria sapeva di terra bagnata ed era ancora umida nonostante non piovesse da ore.

Il traffico newyorkese era più convulso del solito, quindi Tom Tucker decise di raggiungere il "Dixon Hardware & C." in metropolitana. Il vagone era zeppo, per fortuna le fermate da fare erano poche; era abbastanza assorto nei suoi pensieri da non badare al caldo e al tanfo di aria viziata che si venuto a creare. Non aveva tempo. Era determinato a trovare una soluzione a quel problema ed era certo che il "il Paradiso dell'uomo di casa", come recitava il dépliant che teneva in mano, lo avrebbe potuto aiutare. Ma aveva bisogno di staccare: quel pensiero fisso, quella preoccupazione, quel senso d'ansia opprimente che gli faceva ormai compagnia da qualche ora e non aveva intenzione di abbandonarlo, lo avrebbe fatto impazzire. Quindi chiuse gli occhi e tirò un sospiro profondo. Ora però avvertiva l'aria viziata e fece una smorfia di disappunto. Tolse dalla tasca il suo smartphone e aprì una foto di Trisha. L'aveva scattata ieri mentre mostrava la città ai suoi parenti, poco prima di tornare a casa, e gliela aveva mandata per messaggio. Era bellissima come sempre, con quel sorriso timido e quegli occhi sinceri, cui avrebbe affidato la sua esistenza senza esitazione. Aveva una maglia celeste con un ritratto stilizzato al centro. La spallina le cadeva di lato, ma i suoi lunghi capelli neri che profumavano di buono anche in foto, la coprivano. Era la dimostrazione di come l'eleganza fosse una condizione interiore e andasse a braccetto con la semplicità. Tom sorrise e si sentì a casa. Amava quella sensazione. E amava sua moglie.

Il viaggio durò poco. Ripose lo smartphone in tasca e scese dal vagone. Gli sembrò di tornare a respirare dopo una lunga apnea. Prese le scale e fu di nuovo alla luce del sole. Due traverse più là avrebbe trovato il "Dixon Hardware".

Il dépliant manteneva la promessa: quel posto era davvero il paradiso del fai da te e Tom si sentiva come un bambino in un negozio di giocattoli. Non che fosse un appassionato di bricolage, ma frugare lo distraeva. Gli scaffali polverosi del Dixon Hardware lo stimolavano e gli venne spontaneo un sorriso.

Il capannone era stracolmo di gente, il che era normale alla domenica mattina. Tom sapeva che nessuno si sarebbe ricordato di lui, nemmeno i commessi. Tante le facce e tutte diverse. Quella mattina sarebbero passati per quei corridoi sia chi voleva stare al chiuso in previsione di un altro acquazzone, approfittando dell'occasione per vedere dei rubinetti nuovi per la cucina; sia l'hobbista esperto che cercava qualche vernice particolare per un modellino; ma anche il finto hobbista esperto che, di lì a poche ore, avrebbe distrutto casa azzardando un restauro che non era in grado di fare; oppure amministratori di condominio che approfittavano delle offerte; e poi c'era Tom, che cercava un arnese che gli sarebbe servito per far fuori qualcuno.

Tom si aggirava guardingo in mezzo agli scaffali. C'era sì tanta gente, ma proprio in mezzo a loro avrebbe potuto incontrare qualcuno che lo conosceva. Peggio ancora un collega. Teneva la testa bassa come se fosse interessato a qualunque cosa vedesse. Scrutava chi passava con la coda dell'occhio. Non aveva messo un berretto da baseball, quello bianco degli Yankee che usava nelle gite fuori porta, perché pensava che avrebbe dato nell'occhio. Così era solo un cliente titubante che vagava in un megastore senza sapere di preciso cosa comprare.

È per i clienti come Tom che esistono i commessi.

«Posso esserle utile?», fece un ragazzo coi capelli rossi, lentigginoso e con la maglia rossa che riportava lo stemma del negozio.

Tom sobbalzò.

«Uh... mi scusi, ero sovrappensiero», disse

67

pensando a quanto fosse stupido. Tanti accorgimenti per poi farsi sorprendere alle spalle da un commesso che sembrava uscito da "Happy Days". Pensò tra sé e sé: "Sì, mi servirebbe qualche tipo di arma impropria. Cosa mi consiglia?" ma poi optò per un «dovrei... infilare dei chiodi, ma col martello impiegherei troppo tempo...»

Il commesso sorrise: aveva la soluzione.

«Cerca una sparachiodi, quindi.»

«È pratica...?»

«Ormai le fanno piccole e maneggevoli. Sembrano delle pistole.»

Alla parola "pistole" Tom stava quasi per esclamare "La prendo!", ma si trattenne nuovamente.

«Venga, gliele mostro», continuò il commesso.

Tom si trovava già nel reparto giusto, il che lo fece sembrare meno imbranato. Il commesso si mise in punta di piedi e tirò fuori da un ripiano superiore una scatola di plastica da attrezzista. La aprì per rivelare uno strumento che somigliava a un trapano, ma più sottile e meno ingombrante.

«Guardi. Non è un gioiello?». Il tono era quello da venditore d'auto, il carisma un po' meno.

Tom nemmeno la vedeva. Era nuovamente perso nei suoi pensieri. Si chiedeva se quell'attrezzo potesse davvero essergli utile e, ancora, che avrebbe voluto essere lontano da lì. Magari in chiesa con Trisha, invece di organizzare la mattanza di un uomo. Ma "mors tua, vita mea" e tutto quello che riuscì a dire fu «La prendo!». Questa volta a voce alta.

«Bene, l'accompagno alla cassa!» disse il commesso con grande soddisfazione. Si sentì un grande venditore.

Tom pagò e andò via con la sua valigetta. Nessuno

lo avrebbe fermato e nessuno si sarebbe insospettito ma preferì prendere un taxi sino alla Madison. Voleva aria fresca e stanare immediatamente quel grasso uomo dalla faccia di maiale che si aggirava attorno a casa sua per adempiere a una missione senza senso.

Pagata la sua corsa, Tom scese sulla Madison, nei pressi di Central Park. Sistemò la sparachiodi fissandola alla cintura e abbandonò la valigetta in un cassettone. Nessuno badava a lui, e questo gli piaceva. Trovava persino che le strade di New York fossero più sicure del solito.

La folla gli dava un senso di anonimato che sapeva di onnipotenza e che aveva già sperimentato al *Dixon Hardware*. Poteva muoversi in mezzo a quella fiumara senza dare nell'occhio, nessuno si accorgeva di lui, allo stesso tempo però si sentiva parte della città. Sapeva bene che "Faccia di Porco" – ormai aveva preso a chiamarlo così, tra sé e sé – non avrebbe provato a colpirlo in mezzo a così tanti testimoni. Era più al sicuro lì che sul divano di casa sua, con Trisha accoccolata come era solita fare ogni sera, di ritorno dal lavoro, per guardare un episodio della loro serie preferita.

Entrò in uno Starbuck's, il suo posto nei primi mesi newyorkesi, appena arrivato da Long Island.

Prese un cappuccino da portare via, lo pagò e uscì fuori. Lo bevve contemplando ancora quella folla che, con il suo caotico tran tran, sarebbe stata la sua barriera dal killer. Se fosse stato in un film di Frank Capra avrebbe aperto le braccia per poi gridare "Ti amo, New York!", ma pensò che non fosse il caso.

La sparachiodi gli pendeva sul fianco, coperta dal lungo cappotto marrone abbottonato a metà perché non si aprisse. Tra un sorso e l'altro, Tom la toccava per sincerarsi che fosse ancora lì. Pesava. Era la più piccola che aveva trovato, ma era certo che fosse perfetta per l'utilizzo che avrebbe dovuto farne. Ora la sua unica paura era quella che gli cadesse per terra.

Bevve l'ultimo sorso del suo cappuccino e riprese la sua passeggiata alla ricerca dell'avversario. A pochi metri da casa svoltò in direzione di Central Park. Era certo che ripercorrendo i suoi passi – o presunti tali – lo avrebbe incontrato. Se non fosse stato oggi, sarebbe ritornato anche l'indomani.

Tom era come in trance. Il suo stato d'animo, in quei giorni, era quello di chi aveva ritirato delle analisi malevoli. Rischiava di perdere tutto e tante cose gli tornavano alla mente. Sentiva di aver buttato via del tempo, di aver speso troppe domeniche a scrivere e pochi week end di vacanza con sua moglie. Desiderava quel figlio di cui spesso avevano parlato. Si ripromise che se fosse uscito fuori da quella situazione avrebbe preso Trisha e l'avrebbe portata in Europa per una lunga vacanza, da Parigi all'Italia. Niente computer, niente cellulare. Solo lui e lei. E magari sarebbero tornati in tre.

Vagare senza meta a Central Park riossigenava la mente di Tom.

Si chiedeva da quanto tempo non ci andasse e, soprattutto, da quanto non si concedeva una passeggiata con Trisha. Possibile ci volesse un dannatissimo pericolo di morte per fargli riscoprire le piccole cose che avevano sempre amato? Lavoravano troppo e se pure vivessero assieme talvolta era come se stessero a miglia di distanza. Tirò una boccata d'aria.

Toccò nuovamente la sparachiodi: stava ancora lì, ben ancorata sotto il suo cappotto. Ebbe un attimo di esitazione. Cosa stava facendo? Da quando in qua per lui girare armato era una cosa normale?

Pensò nuovamente a quella vacanza con Trisha. Potevano prendersela ora e, magari, non tornare mai più. Quella sarebbe stata la decisione più saggia e migliore. Aria nuova, vita nuova. Al diavolo tutto il resto. Avevano abbastanza soldi per ricominciare da capo da qualche altra parte. Probabilmente avrebbe potuto tenere quella storia per sé e scriverne un romanzo. Sì, ma cosa avrebbe detto a Trisha? Le avrebbe raccontato di quella maledetta telefonata? Del "No way" e del suo odore di sudore misto a birra rancida? Del mefistofelico individuo che, da sotto il cappello, in una nube di fumo, gli annunciava il suo destino? Le avrebbe detto di aver passato la mattina con un arnese da carpenteria nascosto nel soprabito pronto a far fuori un tizio che, in realtà, non gli aveva fatto niente? Non ancora, almeno. Le avrebbe dovuto chiedere di abbandonare tutto e di trasferirsi chissà dove perché era stato selezionato tra tanti come in una macabra lotteria? E poi chi gli garantiva che il killer non lo avrebbe seguito? Quello era un professionista, dannazione, e la gente come lui porta sempre a termine la missione. Lo avrebbe scovato anche in capo al mondo e Trisha sarebbe stata una testimone, a questo punto. Disse ancora nella sua mente: "lei deve starne fuori! Lei deve starne fuori!". Ormai era quasi un mantra.

"Lei deve starne fuori" – ancora una tastata alla sparachiodi. Presente.

"Lei deve starne fuori" – e sentì nuovamente quella boccia nello stomaco che arrivava violenta come un pugno. Doveva sedersi.

Un sassofonista improvvisava un blues. Ora si sentiva in un film di Marlowe. Gli venne da sorridere. Da Frank Capra ad Humphrey Bogart, che salto!

Decise di ascoltare quella session. Il musicista sulla trentina, pantaloni marroni e una felpa che aveva visto giorni migliori, sembrava conoscere bene le sensazioni che frequentavano l'anima di Tom, e le tradusse in note.

Tom, dal canto suo, si stravaccò sulla panchina. Accavallò una gamba, mise un braccio sullo schienale. Mandò un SMS a Trisha.

"Ti penso."

Pochi secondi dopo la risposta: "Anche io. Oops, ho sbagliato numero!" aggiungendo uno smile finale.

A Tom venne da ridere. Erano anni che facevano quel gioco e tutt'ora provava quella punta di divertimento e gelosia mista insieme. Portò la testa indietro e si fece prendere dalle note.

Attorno a lui c'era la vita e questo gli dava sensazioni positive.

Due ragazzi, probabilmente al primo appuntamento se ne stavano seduti due panchine più in là. Ridevano, parlavano, lei gli mostrava l'ultimo libro comprato e lui, impostando la voce, le leggeva l'incipit. Tom chiuse nuovamente gli occhi e, un attimo dopo, nuovamente aperti, i due ragazzi si baciavano. Annuì di approvazione. Due anime si stavano unendo e probabilmente per tanto tempo.

Venne distratto da una madre che si prendeva cura del suo bambino. La donna parcheggiò la carrozzella proprio davanti a lui. Prese il bimbo in braccio e gli pulì il musetto. Lo baciò e lo strinse a sé. Un'altra scena che gli piacque e pensò che sì, sarebbe dovuto tornare spesso al Central Park, ma non da solo. Dopotutto stava a una traversa da casa. La donna rimise il figlio nella carrozzina e riprese la sua passeggiata.

Un gruppo di podisti la superarono. Tom li seguì con lo sguardo. Chissà se aveva ancora il fisico per una corsa all'aria aperta. Sarebbe stato il caso di provare?

Una mano sulla spalla lo fece scattare.

«Mi scusi... non volevo disturbarla...». Il ragazzo sui venticinque anni apparentemente appena uscito dal college, zainetto in spalla e mappa di New York in mano era prevedibilmente un turista.

Tom lo rassicurò con un sorriso, ma non disse niente.

«Sono in vacanza con la mia fidanzata – la ragazza, timida, un po' sciatta ma carina, probabilmente più giovane di lui, abbassò lo sguardo e fece un cenno di saluto con la mano – e mi chiedevo se poteva farci una foto. Sa... vorremmo un ricordo per quando torneremo in Europa.»

L'Europa. Ancora l'Europa. Proprio prima sogna di andarci, persino di viverci, e ora si trovava l'Europa al Central Park.

«Nord Europei?» chiese lui, mentre prendeva la macchina digitale del ragazzo.

«Helsinki», risposte il ragazzo. Il che giustificava il giubbotto legato alla vita, come se quell'autunno newyorkese fosse una calda primavera mediterranea.

«C'è mai stato?»

«No», fece Tom scuotendo la testa. «Ma se un certo affare andrà bene, potrebbe essere la meta della mia prossima vacanza.»

«Si copra bene!», scherzò il ragazzo.

«Contaci!», sentenziò Tom, stimando però che non sarebbe stata la meta migliore per la sua cervicale. Pensò ancora che il Sud Italia sarebbe stata la scelta finale.

I ragazzi si misero in posa e Tom scattò loro qualche foto.

«Ne facciamo un'altra?», chiese lui. Si stava divertendo o, quantomeno, svagando. «Vorrei vi portaste a casa un po' di New York, non di newyorkesi». E guardò sul display quanti passanti aveva catturato con l'obiettivo.

C'erano ancora i due ragazzi. Loro potevano starci: erano teneri, davano una bella immagine del luogo, in una foto fatta a due turisti innamorati. Ma c'era anche un ubriaco che stentava a stare in piedi. Poi ancora dei podisti che passarono davanti proprio mentre scattava e un tizio di spalle che aveva qualcosa di familiare.

Da dietro si notava una chierica che il riporto non riusciva a coprire. Il suo abito era impeccabile e il suo fare indolente come il bulldog che aveva al seguito. Nell'altra mano teneva una busta con poca spesa dentro. Ancora una volta era lui. Ancora una volta nei pressi di casa sua. Ancora una volta immortalato in una foto.

Tom diede la macchina ai ragazzi e si scusò per la fretta.

«Perdonatemi ma mi sono reso conto che sono in

ritardo per un appuntamento.», disse allontanandosi di gran carriera. Poi si voltò:

«Ah, la terza foto è buona. Tenete quella con i ragazzi sulla panchina. Vi somigliano». I due giovani finlandesi rimasero a guardarlo per un attimo.

Tom rallentò. Non voleva dare nell'occhio e non voleva insospettire il suo rivale. Voleva fare in modo di incontrarlo faccia a faccia. Magari parlargli. Capire. Venire a un accordo. E, se fosse stato il caso, fare prima di lui e colpirlo.

L'uomo con la faccia da maiale si fermò di scatto. Anche Tom si fermò, dieci metri dietro a lui. L'uomo estrasse un telefonino dalla tasca e rispose. Parlò a lungo, tenendo il cellulare con la mano con cui teneva il guinzaglio. Con l'altra gesticolava a fatica, per via della busta di nailon. Si accorse di Tom e cambiò espressione. Liquidò il suo interlocutore con "bene, ora devo andare" e ripose il telefono nella tasca dei pantaloni. Guardò Tom con la coda dell'occhio e riprese la sua marcia. Sudava.

Era stato scoperto. Ora il killer sapeva che lui era al corrente di tutto e senz'altra stava già studiando una strategia. Tom doveva agire in fretta. Non aveva tempo di pensare. Doveva fare come ai tempi in Afghanistan, quando alla frontiera si ritrovava i mitra puntati e ogni minimo errore poteva essere fatale. Doveva ragionare d'istinto.

Allungò il passo, tanto ormai era stato scoperto. Voleva raggiungerlo.

L'uomo sudava e dovette rallentare la sua marcia, quasi a fermarsi. Tom era di lì a pochi passi.

L'uomo non trovò di meglio da fare che sorridergli e

salutare.

«Che giornata, vede?», disse lui.

Tom lo guardava con aria severa. Dove voleva andare a parare il grasso maiale?

«Fortuna c'è il vecchio Tommy» - L'uomo indicò il bulldog. Tom ebbe come uno scatto d'ira. Lo sfotteva. Aveva dato il suo nome al cane in segno di spregio. - «I bulldog sono delle belle bestie. Mia moglie dice che mi somiglia. Ma sa, non campano molto. Quindi, appena posso, lo porto a passeggio.»

Il cane si chiamava lui... e sarebbe morto a breve. Era una velata minaccia o un'assurda coincidenza?

Poi l'uomo gli porse la mano.

«Ma non ci siamo presentati... mi chiamo Jeremy Daniel.» Disse l'uomo, che pareva volesse fare amicizia. Tom era titubante, ma accettò il gesto e strinse frettolosamente quella mano moscia e sudaticcia

«Quindi lei non mi sta riconoscendo?» fece Tom.

«Dovrei?» indagò l'uomo, che ora pareva stizzito.

"Sono quello che devi fare fuori", pensò Tom ma si limitò a rispondere: «Tom Tucker. Giornalista. Scrittore»

Il maiale, che ora aveva un nome e un cognome – solo Dio sa se fosse quello vero – accennò un sorriso.

«Mi scusi... sono davvero imperdonabile. Sono certo che per chi fa il suo lavoro non sia il massimo non essere riconosciuto per strada...»

Tom si sentì un'idiota. Qualche passante lo guardava e lui sembrava come l'arrivato che voleva farsi bello con uno sconosciuto.

Jeremy tagliò corto.

«Ora però devo andare. Spero avremo modo di

rincontrarci. Sa, nel mio lavoro il mio motto è "chi non muore si rivede"», disse infilando la mano sotto la giacca per estrarre qualcosa.

Il cuore di Tom prese a battere all'impazzata. Le tempie sembravano non portare il sangue al cervello. Una strana tremarella interna gli faceva cedere le gambe. Lo riportò in sé l'assolo del sassofonista che percepiva in lontananza. Un assolo disperato che sembrava quasi la sirena d'allarme dei bombardamenti.

Ora tutto stava a chi era più veloce.

Tom infilò la mano sotto il cappotto ed estrasse la sparachiodi. Pochi secondi dopo anche Jeremy-faccia-di-maiale prese qualcosa.

Tom puntò la sparachiodi nella fronte dell'uomo e premette due volte il grilletto

- TUMB – TUMB –

Il macabro suono, sordo e cadenzato, pareva l'intro di batteria di un brano rock anni Settanta. Era quasi all'unisono con lo stridente sax il cui suono fluttuava in lontananza.

L'uomo rimase a bocca aperta e cadde.

Cadde a rallentatore o, almeno, a Tom parve così. La sparachiodi rimase ancorata alla mano e, nonostante il braccio gli fosse caduto lungo la persona, non la perse.

Un altro rumore sordo venne prodotto dal grasso corpo che rovinava a terra.

Tommy abbaiò e corse a leccare quella grande faccia sudata.

La busta con la spesa rotolò via mostrando il suo contenuto fatto di due pacchi di spaghetti, del formaggio e dei pomodori San Marzano che tradivano le sue origini italiane. Ancora l'Italia, quella meta tanto sognata e che, ora, vedeva ancora più lontana.

Una donna gridò.

Tom non si voltò. Guardava l'uomo e si chiedeva se fosse davvero così facile. Quindi cercò l'arma che il killer stava estraendo dal fodero che, senz'altro, nascondeva sotto la giacca.

Tra le dita di Jeremy Daniel c'era un biglietto da visita. Il cartoncino stropicciato recitava "Jeremy Daniel – Assicuratore". Seguivano indirizzi e recapiti. In corpo otto lo slogan "chi non muore si rivede".

Tom non capiva più niente. Era una tattica per depistarlo e per poi colpirlo con calma, una volta ottenuta la sua fiducia? Senz'altro era così. Ma poteva anche essere che lui aveva sbagliato persona? Che fosse solo uno sfortunato che somigliava al suo assassino?

Quando Tom fu preso stava ancora lì, a guardare quella salma distesa.

Dal "NY Today" del giorno dopo.

Il supertestimone Sal De Biase è stato ucciso ieri pomeriggio davanti a una folla di testimoni attoniti.

Al momento non si conoscono i legami tra il pregiudicato, oggi nel programma di protezione testimoni, e il suo attentatore, lo scrittore e giornalista Tom Tucker, ma pare non si tratti di un regolamento di conti. L'uomo, armato di una sparachiodi, avrebbe pedinato De Biase per poi finirlo con due colpi alla fronte. Tucker, in stato confusionale, non ha opposto resistenza e si è limitato a dichiarare che "quella faccia di maiale lo avrebbe ucciso".

Sal De Biase, nel programma protezione testimoni da quasi tre anni, ora rispondeva al nome di Jeremy Daniels e faceva l'assicuratore. [...]

L'uomo tirò su la falda del suo cappello di paglia e appoggiò il suo margarita su un tavolino. Nettò la fronte dal sudore con un cleanex e allungò la mano per prendere il cellulare. Il quotidiano che stava leggendo gli copriva le gambe come se fosse un lenzuolo.

Tirò una boccata di fumo da una sigaretta appena accesa, guardò il numero sul display e rispose con abbozzando un sorriso.

«Hai letto anche tu il giornale?» chiese al suo interlocutore, con aria di vittoria.

«Sì» rispose il suo interlocutore. «Pare che avessi ragione: ha funzionato.»

«E nessuno sospetta di noi. Ufficialmente De Biase è stato fatto fuori da un pazzo. Un delitto casuale, senza movente e senza legami con la nostra organizzazione.»

«E se Tucker parlerà?»

«Per raccontare cosa? Che è stato approcciato da un uomo che non esiste e che ora si gode il sole delle Isole Cayman?»

I due uomini risero con soddisfazione. Dopotutto erano loro ad aver vinto la partita in quel gioco perverso fatto di dubbi, paura e morte.

«Goditelo, quel sole» disse l'interlocutore dall'altro capo del telefono.

«Alla faccia tua» aggiunse l'uomo col cappello in tono confidenziale.

Ancora una risata e l'uomo chiuse la comunicazione.

Spense la sigaretta e riprese il suo margarita. Buttò il giornale sulla sabbia e mantenne la promessa fatta: si sarebbe goduto quel sole delle isole Cayman.

Alla faccia di tutti.

Fine

Gianluca Piredda was born in Sassari, in northern Sardinia. His mother was a teacher and homemaker, his father a police officer. As a child, his mother told him stories of Greek mythology instead of traditional fairy tales and, in elementary school, after visiting the office of the local newspaper and he fell in love with telling stories. Not long after he started his journey in publishing. First published at age fifteen, Piredda began working both as an author and as journalist. By 1997 he had published his first comic book miniseries and in 1999 he arrived in the US market, scripting "Winds of Winter" (Antarctic Press, 2000). Since then, he has written numerous books such as "Warrior Nun Areala", "Free Fall", "Airboy", "Spektral" and several short stories for Image Comics. As a journalist, he has worked in radio, TV and for several newspapers and magazines where he served as editor and editor-in-chief. Today Piredda writes articles about pop-culture, current events, travel, and media and for Italian newspapers like Libero.

Michael Hudson is the mastermind behind two boutique-publishing ventures, Sequential Pulp Comics and Raven's Head Press.

He has licensed and worked with King Features, Inc., Condé Nast, C3 Entertainment, Dark Horse Comics, Random House, Edgar Rice Burroughs, Inc., and Frank Frazetta just to name a select few.

His desire has always been to create and publish. He is an accomplished painter and illustrator and has been writing for many years. Michael is the author of four novels all published by Raven's Head Press.

He currently resides in Clearwater, Florida where he continues to write and publish works of fiction that interest him.

Raven's Head Press

Brings you some cool gothic horror